Grasshopper and the Unwise Owl

This title and its sequel *Grasshopper and The Pickle Factory* are available from Granada in hardback

Jim Slater

Grasshopper
and the Unwise Owl

Illustrated by Babette Cole

A DRAGON BOOK

GRANADA
London Toronto Sydney New York

Published by Granada Publishing Limited in 1981

ISBN 0 583 30368 4

First published in Great Britain by
Granada Publishing Ltd in hardback in 1979
Copyright © Slater Books Ltd 1979

Extracts from *Children's Britannica* reproduced
by permission of Encyclopaedia
Britannica International, Limited

Granada Publishing Limited
Frogmore, St Albans, Herts AL2 2NF
and
3 Upper James Street, London W1R 4BP
866 United Nations Plaza, New York, NY 10017, USA
117 York Street, Sydney, NSW 2000, Australia
100 Skyway Avenue, Rexdale, Ontario, M9W 3A6, Canada
PO Box 84165, Greenside, 2034 Johannesburg, South Africa
61 Beach Road, Auckland, New Zealand

Made and printed in Great Britain by
Richard Clay (The Chaucer Press) Ltd
Bungay, Suffolk
Set in Linotype Baskerville

For Elizabeth
who joined a small Wimbledon property company
to find herself in a world of unwise owls and
boastful bats.

Contents

1
Uncle Rudolf's Present

Almost everyone called Graham Hooper, Grasshopper. The nickname suited the young boy well; he was small for his age and very lively.

As he walked home from school that afternoon, he didn't see much of the beautiful countryside. He was too busy kicking a stone and wondering why his mother hadn't given him a dog for his birthday.

'She always said I could have one when I was nine,' he thought. 'I could look after it myself now. She wouldn't have to do a thing.'

Thoughts of a dog were quickly forgotten when a robin flew out of the ivy just in front of him. Grasshopper knew how to find a robin's nest. He walked back a few paces, climbed up the bank a little and slowly crept along searching every inch of the thick ivy. From the higher level he caught sight of the white horse-hairs lining the small nest, in which there were already three tiny white eggs covered with reddy-brown spots. Grasshopper knew that the female would probably be laying a few more, so he made a note of the exact position. In the weeks ahead he wanted to watch the robins bring up their family.

Grasshopper was only a few minutes away from his

home when he decided to eat one of the sweets given to him by his Uncle Rudolf. Everyone said his uncle was a little mad, just because he lived in an old watermill and sometimes did strange things.

Grasshopper smiled as he remembered how friendly the kind old man had become with all the animals in the woods near his home. He had once seen his uncle sitting on his front porch talking to his basset-hound and a heron, and another time he had caught him trying to cheer up a fly.

'You've nothing to worry about,' his uncle had said. 'You should be very proud. All the birds and lots of insects can fly but you're the only one that's actually called "fly".'

The fly seemed to be reassured and buzzed away happily.

Uncle Rudolf had sent his nephew a birthday present – a brown paper bag full of dark green sweets. He had also written a letter. The envelope had been sealed with red wax, and inside there was another much smaller one marked 'SECRET – To Be Read Only By Graham'.

Grasshopper opened his satchel and took out the brown paper bag. Before eating his first sweet he decided to read the letter again. His uncle's spidery writing covered one whole page of his special blue notepaper:

Monday Morning   The Old Watermill

Dear Graham

Here are some magic sweets for your birthday. They will help you talk to animals.

Do not tell anyone else about them being magic. It is our secret.

I hope you will come and stay with me again soon. I have just made friends with a badger who wants to meet you.

Enjoy your birthday, and keep happy.

Love Uncle Rudolf.

P.S. The sweets are very strong so never eat more than one at a time.

Grasshopper picked out a sweet and popped it in his mouth. He was still sucking away as he came to the small muddy path leading from the lane to his garden gate.

'Mm – tastes a bit minty,' he said to himself.

Then Grasshopper suddenly realized that he couldn't see over the ferns that lined the path. Something very strange was happening to him. With every step his body and clothes were shrinking rapidly.

Grasshopper was very frightened. He stopped for a moment to look at his hands.

'They're tiny,' he thought. 'And it hasn't stopped yet. I'd better run home before it's too late.'

He ran as fast as his shrinking legs would carry him.

In another minute he was smaller than the nearby stinging nettles. Grasshopper slowed down to pick his way around a puddle that looked like a huge pond. Back on the path again he realized to his relief that he had stopped getting smaller. Now he was only six centimetres tall and his satchel was less than a centimetre square.

He paused by a daisy to catch his breath. A large animal burst through the thick grass and came running towards him.

'It's bigger than a lion,' he thought in alarm.

Grasshopper tried to hide, but he was so frightened he couldn't move.

2
Sam Snail

The animal was a grey rat. Grasshopper was lucky. It thundered past without seeing him. He suddenly realized that being only six centimetres tall was very dangerous. To him a song-thrush would be as big as a vulture and a fox would seem like a dinosaur.

'Uncle Rudolf didn't say anything about shrinking,' Grasshopper thought. 'The animals are more likely to eat me than talk to me!'

As he stumbled through the grass he felt as if he was deep in the jungle in a distant part of the world. Grasshopper skirted around a dandelion which towered above him like a giant sunflower. After a very tiring five minutes, that seemed more like an hour, he came to a clearing, where he sat down to rest on a large stone.

'I didn't invite you to sit on me,' the stone said as it began to move slowly towards the thicker grass.

'I'm sorry. I thought you were a stone,' Grasshopper replied.

'Of course I'm not. I'm a snail. Please get off my back. I'm in a dreadful hurry.'

Grasshopper stayed put.

'I didn't think snails ever hurried,' he said.

'Usually we don't, but today's different. There's an ants' nest just near here and some of the worker ants might be coming this way. They have a herd of aphids feeding on a nearby plant and they'll be moving them to another one soon.'

'A herd of aphids. What are they?' Grasshopper asked.

'You really are very dim,' the snail observed. 'You don't seem to know anything – you won't last long in these woods. Aphids are a kind of plant lice. The ants look after them like human beings look after cows. They stroke the aphids and out comes honey-dew. It tastes very sweet – ants love it.'

'I'd like to see them,' Grasshopper said.

'That would be very dangerous. You might upset the ants,' the snail warned him. 'They spray a kind of acid that stops you from moving. You want to run for your life but you're paralysed. Then lots of them come and drag you away to their nest.'

The idea of being sprayed with acid and carried off to an ants' nest reminded Grasshopper that he must find his way home as quickly as possible.

'Is this the way to Cherry Cottage?' he asked.

'Yes, it is.'

Grasshopper looked over his shoulder and noticed that there was a thin trail of slime behind them.

'Why do you leave that glistening stuff everywhere?' he asked.

'It helps me move,' the snail explained. 'It's easier to glide over.'

'Wouldn't it be quicker on the path?'

'There you go again. You won't last five minutes on your own. Out in the open I might be seen by a song-thrush. Then he'd swoop down, pick me up in his beak, hit my shell against a stone and that would be the end of me.'

'You all seem to be killing each other.'

'Now you're beginning to understand the problem,' the snail replied. 'I'm a vegetarian myself, but most of the other animals like meat.'

'Do you have a name?' Grasshopper asked.

'Of course. I'm Samuel – but you can call me Sam. All my friends do.'

'Mine call me Grasshopper.'

'That's a silly name. You don't look a bit like a

grasshopper. Come to think of it, I've never seen anything like you before. What are you?'

'I'm a boy who's shrunk. It happened about a quarter of an hour ago.'

Sam Snail showed no surprise.

'I've always wanted to talk to a human being,' he said. 'You might be able to help me.'

'I'll try,' Grasshopper promised.

'Something's been worrying me for a long time,' Sam said. He hesitated then shyly explained his problem.

'Everyone tells me I'm a reptile,' he said in a small voice. 'I hate the idea. It sounds so evil and unpleasant.'

Grasshopper glanced quickly at Sam's shell and his

pinky-grey slug-like body with its two pairs of tentacles.

'I'm sorry, I can't help you, Sam,' he said. 'I'm not quite sure what you are.'

'It's really too much,' the snail complained. 'Jacob the owl didn't know and now even a human being can't help me.'

Sam sighed.

'It seems to me that your brain must have shrunk as well,' he added sharply.

Before Grasshopper could reply, a large shiny black creature came running towards them. It was a beetle, but to Grasshopper it looked bigger than a dog and much more frightening.

'What's that on your back, Sam?' the beetle asked.

'He's a shrunken human, Bertram. Name of Grass-hopper,' the snail replied.

'It was a human who trod on my brother,' Bertram said, giving Grasshopper a nasty look.

'You mean Alfred?' Sam asked. 'I haven't seen him for ages.'

'He won't come out any more,' Bertram explained. 'He's frightened of being trodden on again.'

'Yes, it's very sad,' Sam said. 'Give him my best wishes.'

'Thanks, Sam. I will,' the beetle replied. 'I can't stop and talk now. My wife's ill so I'm doing the house-work. I'm having a terrible day.'

Bertram said goodbye and scuttled off.

'I didn't want to say too much while he was here,' Sam said, 'but Alfred really was squashed by that human. I know it's wrong to joke about other people's troubles, but he's so small now, we all call him the Leetle Beetle.'

'Did he –' began Grasshopper, but Sam stopped him.

'Quiet,' he said. 'Keep very still. Something's coming our way.'

Sam withdrew into his shell. Grasshopper tried to keep calm, but he could hear his heart beating and felt very frightened. He couldn't see anything so he crouched down behind Sam's shell, and waited.

'You're hiding on the wrong side,' a voice sneered from just behind him.

'I said you wouldn't last five minutes in these woods,' was the muffled comment from inside Sam's shell.

Grasshopper looked round in alarm. The beady black eyes of a big dark-grey rat were fixed on him. There was no escape.

3
Rattus Rattus

'Before I kill you, tell me who you are,' the rat said. 'I like to know what I'm eating.'

The rat wasn't joking. In a fight Grasshopper knew he wouldn't have a chance, so he decided to try to keep the rat talking.

'I'll start right at the beginning,' he said.

'There's plenty of time,' the rat agreed. 'I'm not really hungry at the moment.'

Grasshopper began his story, spinning it out as much as possible. When he came to the part about being a human who had shrunk, the rat gave him a nasty look.

'That's why I didn't like you from the start,' it said. 'Humans and rats have always been enemies.'

'That's not true,' Grasshopper protested.

'Oh yes it is. In that horrible poem, the Pied Piper drowned all the rats. You've made "rat" a nasty word. You even call people "dirty rats" when you don't like them.'

'Yes, but we call people "dirty dogs" too,' Grasshopper replied, 'and we love dogs. It's the word "dirty" that's nasty, not "rat".'

'What about the pantomime then?' the rat asked with a sly smile.

'What do you mean?' Grasshopper feared he was falling into a trap.

'The villain is called King Rat. You all hiss and boo him,' the rat said triumphantly. 'You never have a King Dog, do you?'

Grasshopper wasn't going to be beaten.

'I used to have a white rat as a pet. I quite liked him,' he replied.

'There you are. You've made my point,' the rat said. 'If it had been a dog or a cat, you'd have loved him. The best you can say about a rat is that you quite like him.'

Grasshopper had no answer, so he tried to change the subject.

'Where do you live?' he asked.

'Upstairs in the deserted house in the woods.'

'Don't you use the ground floor?'

'No, the brown rats are down there. We black rats like to keep separate.'

'I didn't know there were two kinds of rat,' Grasshopper said.

'There are far more, but black rats and brown rats are the two main ones. Of course, black rats are the best. You humans sometimes call us *Rattus Rattus*. That's a good name, isn't it?'

'Yes, *Rattus Rattus* sounds very strong,' Grasshopper agreed. 'What's your own name?'

There was a slight pause before the rat replied.

'I know it sounds a bit sissy, but my name's Wilfred.'

Wilfred looked anything but a sissy, with his enormous grey body, glittering eyes and sharp teeth.

'You look very tough to me,' Grasshopper said.

'I am,' Wilfred replied proudly, 'and there's another thing. I've already got 105 children.'

'That's amazing.'

'My wife had over fifty last year. Six litters.'

'Fantastic!'

Grasshopper was running out of things to say. But if he couldn't keep talking, he knew he would run out of life too.

'I know what you're doing,' Wilfred said. 'You're asking me all these questions so I won't eat you.'

'Oh no,' Grasshopper lied, 'I'm really interested in everything you're telling me.'

'It won't do you much good,' Wilfred said. 'Not where you're going.'

'Do you believe in heaven?' Grasshopper asked, trying desperately to keep Wilfred thinking about something other than eating him.

'Of course. I believe in hell too. In heaven there's plenty of cheese and milk and bags of corn. In hell there are thousands of cats and rat traps everywhere.'

The thought of going to hell and facing the Great Ratcatcher himself made Wilfred kinder than usual.

'Would you like to say a last prayer before I kill you?' he asked.

'That's very nice of you. Yes, please, I would,' Grasshopper replied.

Wilfred remained silent as Grasshopper began to pray.

Suddenly there was a flapping of wings. Grasshopper

opened his eyes to find that Wilfred had gone. But it wasn't an angel who had come to his rescue – it was a tawny owl.

4
The
Unwise Owl

Talons closed around Grasshopper's arms as he was lifted into the air and carried to a nearby tree. He felt very tiny as he stood on a branch beside the tawny owl, which was over three times taller than he was and had large all-knowing eyes.

'I've never seen anything quite like you before,' the owl remarked.

'I'm a shrunken human,' Grasshopper explained. 'My Uncle Rudolf sent me some magic sweets for my birthday. They were to help me talk to animals, but as you can see, they've made me shrink as well.'

'You might be very small,' the owl said, 'but you have a big problem.'

'What's that?'

'You'll be dead soon, because I'm going to eat you,' the owl replied.

Grasshopper sighed. Fighting for his life was becoming a habit.

'I thought you'd come to rescue me,' he said. 'You look so much kinder than Wilfred.'

'I was just about to catch him when I noticed you. You cost me a rat so you'll have to pay for it.'

'If you let me live, there might be something I can

do for you if I grow to my normal size again,' Grasshopper suggested.

'Such as?' the owl asked.

'I could leave food for you every night.'

'I prefer hunting. It's much more fun and anyway I
love surprises. I had no idea when I came out tonight
that I'd be eating a shrunken human for supper. You'll
be a real treat.'

Grasshopper shuddered at the thought.

'Is your name Jacob?' he asked.

'Who told you that?'

'Sam Snail. He said you didn't know if he was a
reptile.'

'Do you know?' Jacob asked.

'No, but I could easily find out. At home I've got
some books called *Children's Britannica*.'

Jacob fixed his big eyes on Grasshopper.

'It's just possible that I might allow you to go home,'
the owl said. 'But you look very tasty – quite a deli-
cacy in fact – so you'd have to do a lot for me in
exchange.'

'What kind of thing?' Grasshopper asked.

'Information. That's what I want from you,' Jacob
replied. 'You might be my answer to Frederick.'

'Who's Frederick?'

'A pompous young barn owl. He's built quite a
reputation. Nearly everyone goes to him now – they
call him "know-owl".'

'What do they go to him for?'

'Information, of course,' Jacob replied. 'Owls are
supposed to be wise. You have no idea the kind of
things we're asked. The other day a robin wanted to

know the second highest mountain in the world – not
the highest, mark you, the second highest. Frederick
knew it was K2, but I'd never even heard of it.'

'Neither have I,' Grasshopper said.

Then he noticed Jacob look at him sharply.

'I could find out from *Children's Britannica*,' he
said hurriedly. 'They have the answer to everything.'

'What's your name, and where do you live?' the owl
asked.

'I'd better not tell him my nickname,' Grasshopper
thought. 'He seems very serious.'

'Graham Hooper,' he replied. 'I live with my
mother at Cherry Cottage.'

'Hooper,' the owl said, 'I think we can do a deal. I'll let you go if you promise to answer any questions I might ask in future.'

'I agree,' Grasshopper replied, feeling very relieved.

'I try to be fair. I'll take you home now, just to show the kind of owl I am.'

Jacob's passenger climbed on his back and the unwise owl spread his wings and flew him silently home. As they were nearing Cherry Cottage, the owl turned his head.

'Which is your window?' he asked.

Grasshopper leaned forward to point.

'The small one just there.'

Jacob flew straight to the window and perched on the sill while Grasshopper dismounted.

'Jacob, there's something I want to ask you about.'

'Fire away, Hooper.'

'I read somewhere that owls like to eat snails.'

'Yes, they're very tasty.'

'Isn't it a bit risky then for Sam Snail to come and ask you a question? You might just gobble him up instead of answering it.'

'No, Hooper, that wouldn't be polite,' Jacob replied. 'Anyone who comes to me for advice is quite safe. But if I catch them while I'm hunting, that's different. Then I kill them. Mind you, Hooper, I'm quite fond of Sam Snail. I'd have to be terribly hungry to eat him.'

'You're a very kind owl really,' Grasshopper said.

Jacob appeared ill-at-ease and didn't seem to know how to reply. He hopped along to the end of the sill and turned back to look solemnly at Grasshopper.

'I hate sentiment, Hooper,' he said gruffly. 'We have

a business agreement. I brought you back here and you've promised to give me information.'

'Of course I will, but there is a problem, Jacob. If I don't grow again, I won't be able to help you.'

'I took that risk when I didn't eat you for supper. I'd do anything to beat Frederick, so think big, Hooper, think big!'

'Uncle Rudolf will know what to do. I'll ask my mother to phone him.'

'That's a good idea, Hooper, and if you do grow, flash your torch a few times after dark. I'll keep an eye on your window.'

Without another word the owl flew off. Grasshopper walked along the sill and climbed through the open window into his bedroom. While he was wondering how to reach the floor, he felt his heart begin to thump much faster than usual. He looked down at his hands to see if they were growing. For a full minute, nothing happened. Then he noticed that with every heart-beat his fingers were getting slightly bigger. It seemed to be taking a long time, but within three minutes he had regained his normal size and found it easy to step down from the sill.

Grasshopper quickly opened his satchel which, like his clothes, had grown again. He breathed a sigh of relief. The bag of green sweets was still there.

5
Mr Groll's Trickery

Grasshopper looked at his watch.

'Ten to six,' he thought. 'It must last about an hour.'

Quickly he took off his cap and blazer and hurried to join his mother in the kitchen.

'I didn't hear you come in,' his mother said. 'I was getting so worried about you. Your tea's been waiting for over twenty minutes.'

'I'm sorry. I didn't know I was so late,' he replied dreamily.

'You're just like your Uncle Rudolf,' Mrs Hooper complained. 'By the way there's another letter from him. It came by the second post.'

Grasshopper ripped open the first large envelope and then the second smaller one while his mother watched him curiously. The letter was very short.

Monday Afternoon   The Old Watermill

Dear Graham

   I forgot to tell you the sweets might make you shrink for a while.

                    Love Uncle Rudolf

'What's your uncle up to this time?' Mrs Hooper asked.

'It's a secret. I'm not allowed to tell anyone,' Grasshopper replied.

His mother smiled. She knew her brother had a way with children. He made even a letter seem exciting to them.

When Grasshopper had eaten his biscuits and cake and drained his second glass of orange squash, his mother asked him to listen carefully as she had something very important to explain.

'It's bad news, I'm afraid,' she said. 'I've been meaning to tell you about it. After your father died, I signed an agreement to pay five hundred pounds to our landlord, Mr Groll. His solicitor, Mr Leech, came here last month and said that Mr Groll will sue me unless I give him the money.'

'Did you borrow it from him?' Grasshopper asked.

'No. He and that horrible man Cyrus Leech tricked me. Your father once owed Mr Groll five hundred pounds. He paid it all back, but I only found out after I signed the agreement. When I told Mr Groll, he just laughed and said that was my bad luck.'

'You said Mr Groll would sue you. What does that mean?' Grasshopper asked.

'He'll take me to court, where a judge will look at the agreement and hear what we both have to say. If the judge thinks that I owe the money to Mr Groll then we will have to sell everything to pay him the five hundred pounds.'

'The judge might believe what you tell him,' Grasshopper suggested hopefully.

'I'm afraid he won't, because Mr Groll has the agreement he tricked me into signing. The only other person who knows the truth is Mr Groll's housekeeper, Mrs Bevis. She saw your father give the money back but she's frightened of Mr Groll. She made me promise not to bring her into it.'

'Isn't there anything you can do?' Grasshopper asked.

'Only one thing. Mr Leech says that if we move from Cherry Cottage by the end of the month, Mr Groll will give me back the agreement.'

The thought of leaving their home made Grass-hopper realize that his mother was desperate. He knew and loved every corner of Cherry Cottage: his small bedroom, the honeysuckle growing outside his win-dow, the thatched roof, the cherry tree with the black-bird's nest in it, and the wonderful view of the nearby woods.

'Why does he want us to move?' he asked in dismay.

'Because we only pay a small rent. If we leave he can let the cottage for much more or he might even sell it.'

Grasshopper was at a loss for words. He felt like crying, but he had to comfort his mother who was near to tears herself.

'Don't worry,' he said. 'I'm going to ...'

The sight of her son trying to be brave was too much for Mrs Hooper. She fled from the room. Grasshopper didn't follow; he knew his mother wanted to be alone.

He went up to his bedroom to think about the prob-lem. He unpacked his school books and put them in a small pinewood desk. As he emptied his satchel he caught sight of Uncle Rudolf's sweets.

'That's the answer,' Grasshopper thought. 'Now I know what to do. I'll shrink myself tonight and ask Jacob to fly me to Groll Manor. I might be able to get back that agreement.'

6
Flight to Groll Manor

Grasshopper had his bath and got ready for bed.

'I must look up snails first,' he thought.

He took volume sixteen of *Children's Britannica* from the shelf in his bedroom and looked up 'snail'. The second sentence of the article gave him the answer: 'They are gastropod molluscs, which means that the underside of the body is flat and strongly muscular, forming a kind of foot.'

Grasshopper quickly read through the rest of the page.

'Nothing about reptiles. Sam will be pleased. I must remember those words. Jacob will want to know them. Gastropod molluscs ... gastropod molluscs ... gastropod molluscs ...'

Grasshopper kept repeating the words to himself until he knew them by heart. Then he picked up his torch and went to the open window. It wasn't yet very dark outside – he could still see the garden gate.

'He might be watching already,' Grasshopper thought.

He flicked the torch on and off a few times. Nothing happened. He waited ten minutes and tried again. Still no sign of Jacob.

It was becoming darker. Grasshopper leant out of the window and flashed the torch in the direction of the woods.

'Oh dear,' he thought. 'This isn't going to work.'

Suddenly he heard a voice from just outside his window.

'Well, Hooper, what's a snail then?'

Jacob the owl was perched on the window ledge waiting for an answer.

'I'm glad we can still talk to each other. I thought I might only be able to do it when I shrank,' Grasshopper said.

'Once you know how, there's nothing to it, Hooper.'

'I found out that a snail isn't a reptile, it's a gastropod mollusc.'

'Sam will be pleased. It sounds so important. How do you spell it?'

Grasshopper told him, saying each letter very slowly.

'I think I can remember,' Jacob said. 'Now, I've another question. How far away is the moon? Difficult one, isn't it? I was asked last night by a fox. If I don't give him the answer tomorrow, he's going to see Know-owl.'

'Just a moment, I'll look it up.'

Grasshopper took volume eleven, London to Moss, from his shelf. As he flicked through the pages to find 'Moon', Jacob flew from the window and perched on his desk.

'Wait a minute,' he said, 'there's a picture of a moorhen. Will you read that bit to me?' When Grasshopper reached the sentence about moorhens making

a loud croaking sound when frightened, Jacob laughed.

'That's true,' he said. 'I've often heard them do that.'

Grasshopper finished the part on moorhens and turned to 'Moon'. He soon found the sentence he was looking for, and read it aloud: 'The moon's average distance from the earth is actually 384,400 kilometres and its diameter is 3,476 kilometres.'

'It looks much nearer,' the owl muttered.

'Do you understand kilometres, Jacob?'

'Of course I do, Hooper. I've almost forgotten how far a mile is. We went metric a long time ago.'

'Any more questions?' Grasshopper wanted to show Jacob how helpful he was being.

'Not at the moment, Hooper. These books are the answer to Frederick. He won't have a chance now,' Jacob said happily.

'With my help you'll be top owl in the woods,' said Grasshopper.

'Yes, everyone will come to me now.'

'Can I ask you a favour, Jacob?'

'It depends,' the owl replied warily.

'When I shrink again, would you agree to fly me on your back to wherever I want to go? Otherwise it's very difficult for me to get around.'

'You drive a hard bargain, Hooper,' Jacob said after a few moments' thought. 'But I suppose that's fair enough. All right, I agree.'

'Thanks, Jacob. Now I'm going to shrink myself again and I'd like you to fly me to Groll Manor.'

'I didn't expect you to ask me straightaway,' the

owl replied grumpily. 'I don't mind taking you now and then, but I'm not a taxi service you know. I've got other things to do.'

'But you did agree,' Grasshopper insisted.

'I'm an owl of my word. I'll fly you there, but tell me first why you want to go.'

Grasshopper explained his plan.

'It's very risky, Hooper,' the owl commented. 'But I admire courage so I'll help you.'

'Thanks, Jacob.'

'Before we go I want you to know that I don't expect to be called again for at least a week.'

'That's fair,' Grasshopper replied. 'And I'll only give you information when you come to carry me somewhere.'

Ruffling his feathers, Jacob considered the suggestion but didn't mention it again as Grasshopper pulled on his jeans and anorak and fixed his sheath-knife to his belt. When he was fully ready he picked out one of Uncle Rudolf's sweets from the paper bag and began to chew it.

'This really is most interesting,' Jacob said, watching closely. 'Will it take long?'

'About five minutes, I think.'

Grasshopper was right. A few minutes later he began to shrink and was soon only six centimetres tall. He climbed up on Jacob's back and grabbed the owl's neck feathers in his hands.

'I'm ready for take-off,' he said.

Jacob hopped to the window-sill and launched himself into the night air. As they soared above the woods, Grasshopper felt he was moving at tremendous speed.

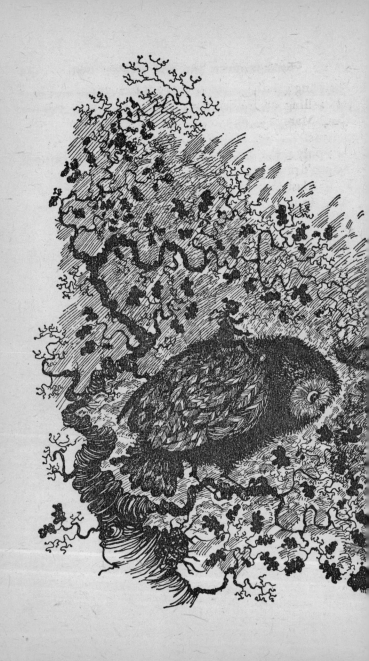

He clung grimly to Jacob's neck feathers to stop himself falling off. When they were about half-way to Groll Manor, Jacob turned his head to speak to Grasshopper.

'I only said I'd take you wherever you wanted to go, I didn't promise to take you back.'

The last thing Grasshopper wanted was a long argument in mid-air.

'Anything you say, Jacob,' he shouted. 'Just get me there safely please.'

They flew the rest of the journey in silence until Jacob settled on a branch of a large oak tree in the garden of Groll Manor. The house was a blaze of light.

'Would you mind taking me to one of the windows?' Grasshopper asked.

'All part of the service,' Jacob replied as he flew from the branch to an open ground-floor window.

'I'll leave you here,' he said. 'Remember, I won't be taking you back.'

'All right, Jacob. But I am surprised. You told me that you were an owl of your word. I didn't think that every little thing in our agreement would matter so much. I trusted you.'

Jacob looked embarrassed, but didn't reply. He waited while Grasshopper climbed down and made sure that he was firmly on the window-sill. Then he flew off without a word. He must have had second thoughts because he swooped back.

'Good luck, Hooper,' he called. 'Watch out for the ginger cat – he's big and nasty.'

7
The
Ginger Cat

Grasshopper was scared by Jacob's warning, but now, even if he wanted to, he couldn't return home. He plucked up courage and stepped through the open window into the house. He walked along the inside sill behind the heavy green curtains and soon found the crack in the middle of them. He peered through; the fat, ugly man sitting in an armchair was clearly Mr Groll. He was wearing a red velvet smoking-jacket. On his lap lay a big ginger cat many times the size of Grasshopper – he seemed like a giant tiger.

'That's your job, Cyrus,' Mr Groll was saying to the man facing him. Grasshopper could only see the back of the visitor's head, but he knew it must be Mr Cyrus Leech, the solicitor.

'There is a way, Nathaniel,' Mr Leech replied. 'We'll threaten to take Roberts to court. He won't be able to afford it and that will force him to sell to you.'

'Once I have his land there will be nothing to stop me,' Mr Groll said. 'I'll get the agreement for you now.'

Mr Groll pushed the ginger cat to the floor and walked over to face an oil painting of some flowers which was hanging over a small table. To Grasshop-

per's amazement the picture swung outwards; behind
it was a safe. Mr Groll twiddled a metal knob and
after a few seconds opened the steel door.

'That's where my mother's agreement will be,'
Grasshopper thought.

'This is the one,' Mr Groll said, handing Cyrus

Leech a thick piece of white paper with a large blob of red sealing-wax on it.

'Thanks, Nathaniel, I'll write Roberts a letter first thing tomorrow.'

'Before you go, I'd like your opinion on a painting I bought yesterday.'

'Knowing you, I'm sure it's a bargain,' the solicitor laughed.

Cyrus Leech rose from his chair; he was very thin with iron-grey hair and bushy eyebrows. Grasshopper was surprised to see that he towered above Mr Groll as the two men left the room together.

'What a bit of luck,' Grasshopper thought. 'I must hurry and get into the safe before Mr Groll comes back.'

He ran along the window-sill and quickly found the gold cord that opened and closed the curtains. He had been taught to climb ropes at school so it was no problem for him to find his way down to the floor. The ginger cat was lying by the side of Mr Groll's chair, blinking sleepily at the fire.

'What a horrible-looking cat. Thank goodness he hasn't seen me yet.' Grasshopper ran across the brown carpet. It had a thick pile which came up to his ankles and made him feel as if he was running through heather.

Grasshopper stopped under the small table.

'I can't climb up those legs,' he decided. 'They're too smooth and shiny.'

Then he noticed the wainscotting that ran at waist height like a sill round the room.

'If I can get up there I could walk along it until I'm

under the safe.' Grasshopper glanced nervously at the cat's back as he searched for the best way to reach the sill.

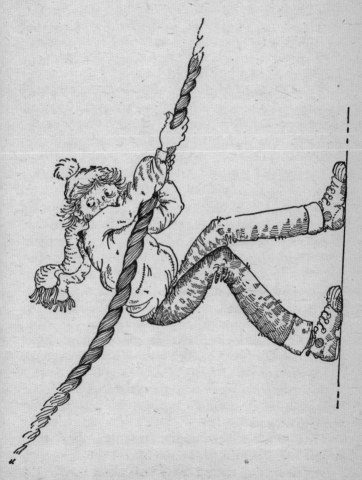

'That looks as though it might do,' he thought, as he noticed some flex in the corner of the room.

He ran over and grabbed the flex in both hands. Bracing his legs against the wall, he began the long climb. Grasshopper found it very hard work and had to pause for breath when he was only half-way up.

'There's no time to lose,' he told himself. 'Mr Groll might come back any second.'

It took Grasshopper another three minutes to reach the top. The light green wallpaper was very smooth and the narrow sill was covered in a glossy cream paint. He began to edge forwards but found it much too slippery.

'I'll be safer on hands and knees,' he decided. 'But I mustn't look down, it might make me dizzy.'

Grasshopper crawled the rest of the way until he was under the safe. He stood up and found that if he stretched he could just reach the edge of the open door. He hauled himself up and climbed inside. To Grasshopper it looked like a giant black cave and was much deeper than he had expected. There was a small pile of papers in the safe, a green metal box and several large packets of twenty-pound notes.

'I haven't much time,' Grasshopper thought. 'If Mr Groll comes back now he might close the safe door.'

The fear of being trapped gave Grasshopper extra energy. He clambered over the papers and checked the signature on the top one. It wasn't his mother's. He found it difficult to pull the first agreement far enough away to give himself a clear view of the next one. He managed it at last, but again the name was someone else's.

'Oh dear, I must have been in here five minutes already. I daren't stay much longer.'

Grasshopper had a quick look into the sitting-room. There was still no sign of Mr Groll, so he went back

inside the safe and pulled the second agreement away from the small pile. The third one didn't look important enough, as it was only a single piece of paper. There was a sixpenny stamp on it, but no red wax. Then he glanced at the signature on the bottom and felt a surge of joy.

'That's Mum's. This is the one. I must get it out of here and hide before Mr Groll comes back.'

Grasshopper dragged the piece of paper to the entrance. He peered out. Mr Groll still hadn't returned. Grasshopper rushed round to get behind the agreement and then he began to push it out of the safe. When it was half-way the piece of paper suddenly fluttered down to the floor. Grasshopper lowered himself over the edge of the open doorway until he felt the sill under his toes. Once he had a firm foothold he crawled well away from the safe and hid behind the top of some flowers, which were in a vase on a nearby side-table. He looked out from his hiding-place and tried to spot the piece of paper. It was half hidden under the armchair Mr Leech had been sitting in.

'That's good. Mr Groll might not see it there.'

But the ginger cat had heard the paper fluttering to the floor. He sensed there was something small and alive in the room. Tom was a very clever cat. He pretended to be asleep, but his eyes were just open and he was listening for the slightest sound.

8
The
Blazing Forest

Mr Groll returned from the hall, closed the safe and with a sigh sank into his armchair. Mrs Bevis followed him into the room and waited by the door. She coughed nervously, but Mr Groll didn't bother to look up from the papers he was studying.

'What do you want?' he asked.

'I wondered if you would like some more coffee, sir?'

'No. You can go to bed now,' he said sharply.

Mrs Bevis quietly left the room.

Grasshopper crouched on his hands and knees again and crawled along the sill back to the flex in the corner. He grabbed it in his hands and began to climb down to the floor. When he reached the carpet he looked anxiously at his watch.

'Only a quarter of an hour left before I grow again,' he thought. 'I'll never manage to get the paper out of this room. I must find a way of destroying it. The fire's the answer – I'll try and pull the paper to the hearth. The cat looks as if he's still asleep.'

In fact Tom was very wide awake. He had heard something climb down the flex and was lying in wait hoping that whatever it was would come near enough for him to pounce.

Grasshopper ran across the thick carpet until he reached the agreement lying beneath the armchair facing Mr Groll. He grabbed the piece of paper with both hands and began to drag it away from under the chair. He was surprised that Mr Groll and the cat didn't seem to have heard. Mr Groll was still busy studying his papers, but Tom now knew Grasshopper's exact position. He could afford to wait; his unknown enemy was coming nearer.

Grasshopper pulled the paper towards the blazing logs. They were six times taller than he was and looked to him like a forest that had caught fire. As he reached the front of the armchair he realized he would have to risk going into the open and being seen by Mr Groll and the ginger cat. There was a metre and a half between the chair and the fire.

'It's now or never,' Grasshopper realized. He began to drag the paper across the gap. As he came nearer to the fire he broke into a sweat. The heat was too much for him; he could hardly breathe. He ran back to the other side of the agreement and tried to push it from behind.

'It won't move,' he thought. 'I know, I'll swing the paper round.' Grasshopper grabbed the corner and ran towards the hearth. The paper ended up a little nearer the fire. Grasshopper scampered back, grabbed a corner again and whirled it round. Slowly the paper came closer to the fire until it was only twenty centi-metres away.

Grasshopper was working so hard that he didn't notice Tom turn his head. The cat's large green eyes glistened as he saw his prey. He hesitated for a few moments; he had never come across anything quite like Grasshopper before.

Grasshopper was so close to the fire that he had to push the paper the last few centimetres. On the smooth tiled surface of the hearth it was much easier, but still a slow job. He was just wondering if he could last any longer when the edge of the agreement caught alight and burst into flame. Grasshopper ran for cover.

Tom decided to wait no longer. He sprang into action and hurled himself across the carpet. Grasshopper scurried under the armchair.

The cat lay on the carpet, his cruel green eyes glaring at Grasshopper. Suddenly he reached out and tried to slash the boy with his claws.

'You won't escape from there,' he hissed. 'Now I'm

going to make so much fuss Mr Groll will come and move the chair. Then I'll kill you.'

'Jacob said you were big and nasty,' Grasshopper replied. 'He was right. I can't remember ever having seen an uglier-looking cat.'

Grasshopper had made up his mind. If he was doomed to die, he would go down fighting and there was just a chance that he could make Tom very angry. Then the ginger cat might do something silly and Grasshopper could escape.

It was as if Tom had read his mind.

'You won't make me lose my temper,' he said.

'How can you be so sure, ugly-face?'

'Because I'm a cool cat,' Tom replied with a smug smile.

Tom would soon attract Mr Groll's attention. The cat's paw kept sweeping under the chair, its claws at full stretch. Grasshopper looked round desperately and suddenly caught sight of a small greyish-brown figure waving to him from a little hole in the wall.

It was a house mouse, no further than two metres away from the other side of the chair.

Grasshopper decided to make a dash for it.

'You're so fat and lazy,' he said to Tom, 'it doesn't surprise me that there are so many rats in this house.'

He glanced to one side of Tom and tried to make the big cat think that he had just seen something move. Tom knew it was probably a trick but couldn't resist having a quick look round. That was enough for Grasshopper; he dashed out from under the chair and sprinted across the carpet to the mousehole.

Although Tom was taken by surprise, he was after him in a flash. The house mouse vanished and Grasshopper just managed to get inside the hole as Tom's claw raked out at him.

'That was a narrow squeak!' the mouse said.

As Grasshopper gathered his breath, he looked around the inside of the mousehole. It was about the size of a shoe box, with plenty of room for both of them.

The mouse didn't seem to be worried about the ginger cat outside.

'Tom won't get you in here. He's been trying to

catch me for years,' the mouse said. 'I don't know who you are but any enemy of Tom's is a friend of mine.'

'I'm called Grasshopper. I'm a shrunken human and I've come here on a special mission.'

'That sounds very exciting,' the little mouse exclaimed. 'My name's Albert. I bet you thought it was Jerry, didn't you?'

Grasshopper couldn't help laughing. Albert was full of fun and seemed very keen to help.

'I've a big problem,' Grasshopper explained. 'In a few minutes' time I'll start growing again.'

'You can't stay in here, then. It might ruin my home,' Albert said in dismay.

'Maybe if Tom saw me growing, I could frighten him away?'

'He's easy to fool,' Albert agreed. 'I often do it just for fun.'

Grasshopper decided to try.

9
Captured

When, a few moments later, his heart began to pump faster Grasshopper knew that he would soon start growing again.

'Thanks for your help,' he said to Albert as he went to the entrance of the mousehole.

'I'm getting bored with this,' Grasshopper called to the cat. 'I've decided to put a stop to it by killing you.'

Tom laughed.

'Watch me carefully,' Grasshopper said. 'I'll start growing in a few seconds. When I'm five times bigger than you are, I'll finish you off for good.'

Tom was surprised by his prey's confident manner. The cat didn't reply but his cruel green eyes followed every move.

'I suggest you watch my hand,' Grasshopper said. 'You'll get the idea better that way.'

Tom switched his attention to Grasshopper's hand and to his amazement it began to grow. The cat moved back from the mousehole. Grasshopper was still growing fast and he had to get out before it was too late. He tried to look as confident as possible.

'Now I'm going to give you a lesson you'll never forget,' he called to Tom.

While the ginger cat watched, Grasshopper doubled in size. Tom retreated. The strange little animal crawled out of the mousehole into the room. Tom wondered if he should attack while he was still bigger than his new enemy, but he had waited too long. Now the strange animal was standing on its hind-legs, just like a human being, but only a quarter of the size. A minute later it was twice as big. Tom gave a squawk of alarm and raced round to his master's side.

Mr Groll looked up from his papers. He had been half conscious of something going on for some time.

'What's wrong, Tom?' he asked. 'Have you found a mouse?'

He heaved himself out of his armchair. As he did so, to his amazement, he caught sight of a curly-haired young boy in a blue anorak standing quietly behind the other armchair.

'Who the devil are you?' Mr Groll shouted.

'Hooper,' Grasshopper replied nervously. 'Graham Hooper.'

'How did you get in here?'

'Through the window.'

'Are you the son of Mrs Hooper of Cherry Cottage?' Mr Groll barked at him.

'Yes, I am.'

'Why did you break into my house?'

Grasshopper heard himself blurt out the answer.

'To get the agreement you tricked my mother into signing.'

Mr Groll suddenly remembered the safe door had

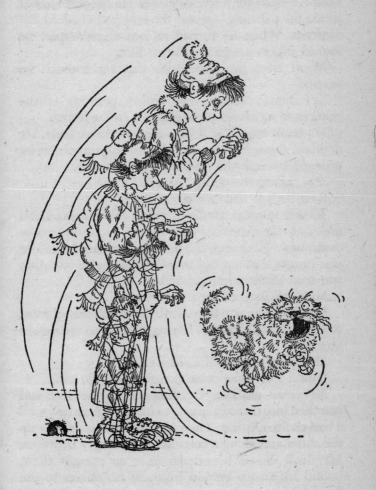

been left open for a few moments. He quickly walked to the oil painting, opened the safe and checked the contents. When he turned to face Grasshopper, he looked angry enough to strangle him.

'What have you done with that agreement?' he snarled.

'It's there,' Grasshopper replied, pointing to the remains of a charred piece of paper in the hearth.

Mr Groll looked as if he was about to explode. He grabbed the telephone and dialled a number. As he waited for a reply he turned to Grasshopper.

'I'm calling the police,' he said.

Grasshopper had no time to reply.

'I want to speak to the officer in charge,' Mr Groll said into the receiver. There was a pause before he continued. 'Nathaniel Groll of Groll Manor here. I've just caught a young boy breaking into my house. Can you send someone immediately?'

Mr Groll listened for a moment.

'All right,' he said impatiently, 'but tell the sergeant to hurry. It's a nuisance having to keep an eye on the boy.'

Mr Groll replaced the receiver.

'You'll soon have cause to regret this,' he said.

Mr Groll grabbed Grasshopper by the arm and marched him through into the kitchen, where he found a ball of thick string. Then he pushed Grasshopper up the stairs and along a corridor to an empty bedroom. Mr Groll shoved him down on to an upright chair, bound his hands behind him and his ankles to the front legs.

'The police sergeant will be here in an hour,' Mr

Groll said. 'I suggest you use the time to think how stupid you've been.'

Mr Groll slammed the door behind him and stumped down the stairs.

'Oh dear,' Grasshopper thought. 'I'm in real trouble now. They might send me to prison for years. I must try to escape.'

Grasshopper tested the strength of the thick string, but he was still unable to move. A few minutes passed before he noticed the brass handle turn slowly. Mrs Bevis quickly came inside and closed the door behind her.

'You poor boy,' she said. 'I wish I could help you.'

'You could loosen the string a little,' Grasshopper suggested. 'It's cutting into me.'

'I'd love to let you go,' Mrs Bevis replied, 'but I daren't. He'd kill me if he found out.'

'I won't tell anybody,' Grasshopper promised.

Mrs Bevis slackened the string around Grasshopper's wrists. It still held him securely but allowed a little more movement.

'Thanks, that's much better,' Grasshopper said.

'I wish I could do more,' Mrs Bevis mumbled, as she hurried away.

As Grasshopper struggled to free himself his arm brushed against a small bulge in his anorak pocket.

'I wonder if I can reach Uncle Rudolf's sweets,' he thought. 'Then I can shrink myself out of this string and escape.'

10
The
Boastful Bat

Grasshopper twisted his hands round as far as possible to find that he could just reach his pocket. He felt for the top of the paper bag and after a minute's fumbling managed to grip a sweet between his fingers. He brought it out carefully, bent his head down and tried to pop the sweet into his mouth. There was a ten-centimetre gap. He strained so hard that the string cut into his wrists and his fingers began to feel numb, but the gap still remained. Then Grasshopper noticed a small wooden side-table near to him.

'I'll put the sweet on that,' he thought. 'I'll be able to get at it more easily.'

The idea worked. Grasshopper found that when he bent his head down he could just reach the table. As soon as the sweet was in his mouth he began to chew it. The mint flavour was very pleasant, but he had no time to linger. He needed to shrink as quickly as possible and escape from Groll Manor.

Within two minutes Grasshopper was small enough to shrug off his bonds. While he waited for the shrinking to finish he moved over to the window, which was just ajar. A few moments later he began to climb up the curtain cord. When he reached the sill he swung across to it and stepped out into the night air.

Grasshopper looked down. Although the lawn was only five metres below him, he felt as if he was standing on the top floor of a skyscraper. He nearly lost his balance when he was startled by a thumping noise. The young boy looked up to see a large tiger-moth, attracted by the light, battering its head against the window.

'Excuse me,' Grasshopper said. 'I wonder if you can help me?'

'Can't you see I'm busy?' the moth replied.

'Yes, but what you're doing seems rather pointless to me.'

'I know I'm being silly, but we moths always do this. If you'd switched the light off before you came out, I could have helped you. But you didn't, so I'll have to stay here now.'

After that the moth ignored Grasshopper and carried on banging his head against the window.

'I can't climb down,' Grasshopper thought. 'I need help from something that flies. Oh, I do wish Jacob was here.'

Grasshopper was startled by a squeaking noise. Something flew near to him and veered away with another squeak.

'I'm off,' the moth said. 'That was a bat. They eat moths.'

It vanished without another word. The bat squeaked again and swooped even closer to the window.

'What are you then?' the bat called out to Grasshopper.

'I'm a shrunken human,' he replied in a loud
voice. He wanted to sound big, tough and difficult to
digest.

Grasshopper drew his knife, but after a moment's
thought put it back in the sheath. The knife had
shrunk with him and was a pitiful weapon against the
bat, which had a wing span twice as big as Grasshopper
himself.

Grasshopper already knew that like human beings
most animals enjoy talking about themselves.

'Are you blind?' he called. 'We sometimes say
people are as blind as bats.'

The bat flew to a nearby oak tree and hung up-
side down from a branch.

'My eyes may be weak,' it replied, 'but I use something far better. I have a radar system. I can tell just
where insects are, which way they are flying and, most
important of all, if I can eat them.'

'How does your radar work?' Grasshopper asked.

'I squeak a few times and with my big ears I can
tell from the echoes exactly where things are. Clever
stuff, don't you think?'

'Very.'

'There's another thing,' the bat called to him. 'I
know you think I'm a bird, but I haven't got any
feathers at all. I'm a mammal just like you, but there's
one big difference between us.'

'What's that?'

'I'm much better looking!' the bat replied, squeaking with laughter.

Before Grasshopper could say a word, the boastful bat continued.

'Did you know that bats are the *only* mammals that can fly? You can't fly, can you? Quite something, isn't it?'

'It certainly is. Would you mind showing me? I'd like to get down to the lawn.'

'Of course I will,' the bat said with a toothy smile. 'One of the many things I so admire about myself is my kindness to others.'

The bat flew over to join Grasshopper and hung from the window-sill.

'Climb on my back and I'll take you down,' it said.

Grasshopper was surprised to find that the bat's body was a little smaller than his own – only the wings made it look bigger.

'Thanks for your help,' he said when they reached the lawn below.

'We mammals must stick together,' the bat squeaked as it flew off into the night.

Grasshopper wondered what to do next.

'If only Jacob was here,' he thought. 'Everything would be all right.'

At that moment he heard someone slam the front door of Groll Manor. Grasshopper remembered what Sam Snail had said to him about the dangers of being in the open. He searched for cover. The uncut lawn rose around him like a field of green corn. He waded through it towards a clump of bushes about three metres away.

He was almost there, when, in the moonlight, he

suddenly caught sight of the fearsome figure of Tom the cat coming round the corner of the house. Grasshopper froze in his tracks.

11
Billy the Poet

'I know you're in the garden,' the ginger cat said in a loud voice, 'and this time I'll kill you.'

Grasshopper crouched down in the long grass.

'If you give yourself up, I won't torture you,' the cat hissed. 'Just one quick bite and it'll be all over.'

Tom was coming nearer, his tail swishing angrily as he carefully searched the ground to left and right. The ginger cat knew he was close to his prey. Grasshopper began to crawl through the grass towards the bushes, which were now only a metre away.

A soft whisper broke the silence.

> 'If you want to escape the cat of Groll,
> May I suggest you use my hole.'

Grasshopper risked a quick look over the top of the grass and saw a brown rabbit beckoning to him from under the bushes. Tom was now very close. There was no time to be lost – he stood up and ran as fast as he could towards the rabbit. Luck was on his side; Tom didn't see him until it was too late. Then with an angry miaow he leapt after his enemy, but Grasshopper was already safely inside a large rabbit hole.

Two huge green eyes gazed down after him.

'I just knew you were in the garden,' the cat hissed. 'I can wait here all night. You'll have to come out when you want to grow again.'

Grasshopper looked nervously at his watch. There was still half an hour left. The brown rabbit spoke in a soft friendly voice:

> 'My name's Billy,
> I know it's silly,
> I talk in rhyme,
> All the time.'

'Thank you for saving me,' he replied. 'My friends call me Grasshopper.'

Billy looked a little worried and there was a long silence before he answered.

> 'It really is a terrible shame,
> Nothing will rhyme with your name.'

(In fairness to Billy, it should be pointed out that three days later he thought of 'Gobstopper'.)

'Don't worry about that,' Grasshopper said. 'I've a much bigger problem. Is there any way of escaping from here?'

Billy didn't reply for a moment. He was busy thinking of his next rhyme.

> 'This warren belongs to Cecil, my brother,
> You've come in one hole,
> You'll go out of another.'

Grasshopper breathed a sigh of relief.

'Will it take long?' he asked. 'I must hurry. I've got less than half an hour.'

> 'It is my boast,
> When I am host,
> Guests nothing lack,
> Climb on my back.'

the rabbit said with an inviting smile.

Grasshopper scrambled up Billy's side and gripped the fur just behind his neck.

'I'm ready,' he called.

He didn't bother to shout goodbye to Tom; he much preferred to leave the cat sitting outside the hole all night.

Billy raced at high speed through the dark warren, twisting and turning so much that Grasshopper soon

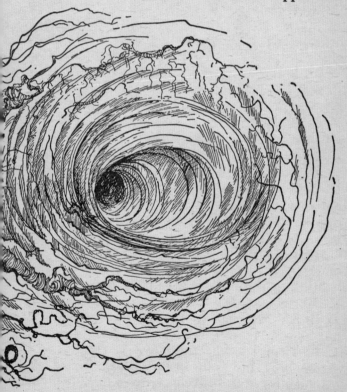

felt as though he was in a maze. Ten minutes later, the rabbit slowed down a little and began to climb again to ground level. They turned a sharp corner and suddenly came into a part of the warren well lit by the moon shining down the opening ahead of them.

When they left the rabbit hole Grasshopper was disappointed to find they were still in the gardens of Groll Manor. The rabbit had only carried him as far as the fishpond, about two hundred metres away from the house.

Grasshopper dismounted but before he could thank Billy, the rabbit had disappeared down his hole. He was still wondering why the friendly poet had departed so abruptly when something very large swooped down at him. Jacob the owl had returned.

'Am I glad to see you,' Grasshopper said as Jacob alighted on the ground beside him.

'I've come back, Hooper, because I wanted to make sure about the distance to the moon,' Jacob said. 'I must get it absolutely right. Three hundred thousand and something, wasn't it?'

Grasshopper thought quickly. 'If I tell him now, he might fly off.'

'Take me home and we can check with the encyclopaedia again,' he suggested.

Much to his surprise, Jacob made no complaint.

'All right, Hooper,' he said. 'You can board now. Jacob Airlines announce the departure of Flight JA 423 from Groll Fishpond to Cherry Cottage.'

Grasshopper laughed happily as he climbed up on Jacob's back. Just as the owl was about to take off, a soft voice called to Grasshopper from the rabbit hole.

'Goodbye, young Hooper,
Meeting you was super.'

Grasshopper turned and waved. 'Goodbye Billy, and thanks for everything.'

'He may be a William, but he'll never be a Shakespeare,' Jacob said dryly as they soared over the woods.

Jacob flew so fast that Grasshopper had to wait until he was back safely on his bedroom window-sill before speaking to the tawny owl again.

'Tell me, Jacob,' he asked. 'How did you find me?'

'You don't know much about owls, do you, Hooper?' Jacob replied. 'Even if I say so myself, we really are quite remarkable birds. We can see every detail of the smallest things we fly over at night.'

'But you didn't know I'd be so far away from the house.'

'You mustn't interrupt, Hooper. The other thing about owls that will amaze you is their hearing. When I'm up a tree I can hear the rustling of a mouse moving in the grass below. I heard that rabbit come out of its hole. I quite enjoy eating rabbits, you know.'

Grasshopper always felt a little uneasy when Jacob began to talk about eating other animals.

'I'd better go in now,' he said. 'As soon as I've grown again, I'll look up "Moon" and let you know the distance.'

'You needn't bother, Hooper. I've just remembered – it's 384,400 kilometres.'

Grasshopper was surprised that Jacob knew, but he didn't ask the unwise owl what had jogged his memory.

'Thank you very much for bringing me home,' he said.

'It was kind of me,' Jacob replied. 'Now I don't want to hear from you for another week. I need a rest after all this excitement.'

'Anything you say,' Grasshopper agreed wearily.

'One more thing, Hooper. Did you get what you went for?'

'Yes, I did, Jacob.'

'Well done, Hooper,' the tawny owl said, before gliding away.

As he climbed through into his bedroom Grasshopper couldn't help wondering if the unwise owl had ever really forgotten the distance to the moon.

12
The Hoot
of an Owl

Grasshopper had no idea what might happen to his clothes if he took them off while he was still tiny. He decided to wait until he had grown again before he undressed.

Fifteen minutes later, he had just got into bed when he heard a loud knocking on the front door. Mrs Hooper opened it to find Mr Groll and a police sergeant standing outside.

'Do come in,' she said. 'Is anything wrong?'

'There certainly is,' Mr Groll replied. 'Your son broke into my house tonight and destroyed the agreement you signed.'

'What nonsense!' Mrs Hooper replied. 'Graham's upstairs in his bed fast asleep.'

'I'm sorry about this, Mrs Hooper,' the red-faced police sergeant said. 'Mr Groll's made a complaint and we have to look into it.'

'That's all right, Sergeant. I know you have your job to do,' she replied.

'There's a very easy way of finding out the truth,' Mr Groll said slowly. 'Let's see if your son is in his bedroom.'

'That's a good idea, sir,' the police sergeant agreed.

'If the boy was at Groll Manor, he couldn't possibly have beaten your car back here.'

'I don't like to waken Graham at this time of night,' Mrs Hooper protested.

'She's playing for time,' Mr Groll said with a sneer.

'It seems to me that this is the only way to prove your son is innocent,' the sergeant pointed out.

Mrs Hooper thought for a few moments. She didn't like Mr Groll bringing the police to her house and was anxious to prove him wrong.

'I don't want to alarm Graham,' she said. 'I'll go first to let him know that you want to see him.'

The two men agreed, so Mrs Hooper went up to her son's bedroom.

'Who was that knocking at the door, Mum?' Grasshopper asked.

'Mr Groll and a police sergeant, Graham. They want to have a word with you.'

Grasshopper didn't reply. He pretended to be sleepy. Mrs Hooper stood by the door and called down to her visitors.

'Here he is. Safe and sound in bed.'

Mr Groll couldn't believe his eyes. He switched on the light and walked over to the bed.

'How did you get here?' he asked.

'I flew on the back of an owl,' Grasshopper replied.

The police sergeant and Mrs Hooper both laughed.

'He's still dreaming,' the sergeant said. 'I think we should let him go back to sleep.'

Mr Groll glared at Grasshopper. He went red in the face and then stomped out of the room.

'Goodnight, Graham,' his mother said.

When the door had closed behind them, Grass-hopper snuggled down in his bed. He was very tired and full of happy thoughts, as he drifted off to sleep.

'That settles it,' the police sergeant said. 'I'm sorry to have disturbed you and your son, Mrs Hooper. We won't take up any more of your time.'

Mr Groll didn't say another word. He knew that he

was beaten, and without the agreement he wouldn't be able to force Mrs Hooper and her son to leave Cherry Cottage.

As Mr Groll and the police sergeant walked down the path to the front gate, they heard a strange noise:

'Hoooo ... hoooo ... hoooo ...'

The sergeant looked up into a nearby beech tree.

'Look, sir,' he said pointing. 'You can see quite

clearly from here. It's a tawny owl – sounded just as if it was laughing at us.'

Before Mr Groll could reply, the owl hooted again: 'Hoooo ... hoooo ... hoooo ...'

What Grasshopper's Children's Britannica told him about the animals

Ant. The most important thing about an ant is that it does not live alone as most other insects do. The ant running about on the path is one of a family and sooner or later will return to a nest and join its companions.

The common black garden ants and many others live in nests built in the ground or under stones or roots. There are a vast number of compartments or separate rooms, all connected by a labyrinth or network of galleries.

There are three sorts of ant in a colony – a queen, workers and males. A queen is a perfect female which can lay eggs, but most of the females cannot normally do this and are the workers of the colony. They build the nest, search for food and look after the grubs.

Aphid Great numbers of these little insects can be seen on the leaves, stems and roots of many plants. The aphid uses its beak to suck the sap from a plant, but it takes more than it needs and the rest, only slightly altered, is passed out through the insect as honey-dew.

Ants have found that if they stroke the aphids with their feelers the aphids will produce tiny droplets of honey-dew for them to lap up. They even protect them by building shelters over them and at times they herd them together or take them to the ant colonies just as if they were cattle.

Extracts from *Children's Britannica* © Encyclopaedia Britannica International, Limited 1978.

Bat Of all mammals, big and small, the bats are the only ones that fly. Several different mammals have developed membranes (sheets of skin) between their fore and hind legs on which they can glide from tree to tree, like the flying squirrels, but only the bats truly fly. Their long arms and their hands, with specially long fingers, are covered with very thin membrane and make efficient wings. The membrane extends to the tiny legs and in many kinds to the tip of the tail as well.

With these wings bats can steer a very accurate course, avoiding any obstacle which may lie in their path. Experiments have shown that they can do this even when blindfolded and it has been proved that they tell where objects are by means of the echoes they hear when they send out very high-pitched sounds.

Beetle Beetles are to be found in almost any place where animals exist, except in the sea. True beetles have the scientific name of Coleoptera, which means sheath-winged, and they all have one thing in common: what should be the front pair of wings are not wings at all, but thick, usually tight-fitting sheaths, or covers (called *elytra*), which completely cover the real pair of wings and so protect them. Only beetles have sheaths like this and they usually meet in a straight line down the middle of the back.

When a beetle flies, it lifts up its wing covers and then spreads out the wide, thin wings behind them. All beetles were, at one time, flying insects but many of them, like the common ground beetles, have given up flying and depend on their six legs for travelling about.

Cat The cat belongs to the same family of animals as the lion, tiger, jaguar and leopard.

Though a cat cannot see in total darkness it can see in the dark far better than human beings. If you examine a cat's eyes in a bright light you will see that the pupils in the centre become smaller until they are mere slits. If you could look at the pupils in the dark, you would find that they had grown round and large so as to receive all the light available. A cat is helped, too, when it is moving about in the dark by its whiskers, which act as feelers. It usually stalks its prey, hiding among the branches of a tree or in undergrowth and then springing on it.

The cat is a solitary animal and does not accept a human master as completely as does a domestic dog. Because of this it does not become so dependent on man and a cat will return to a wild life more quickly than other domestic animals.

Moth About 120,000 species or kinds of moths are known to scientists, there being many more species of them than butterflies.

Like all small living creatures, moths have plenty of enemies always ready to prey on them. At night they are greedily eaten by bats and owls, but nevertheless they are far safer by night than by day. This perhaps explains why it is that there are such enormous numbers of kinds that only fly at night, for those that acquired this habit stood a much better chance of surviving and, therefore, of breeding.

The tiger moths are gaily coloured moths that sometimes fly by day. The common tiger moth of Britain has dark markings on the yellow forewings and scarlet hindwings. Its caterpillar has a furry dark coat and is known as a 'woolly bear'.

Mouse The best known mouse is the house mouse, so called because it lives where there are human beings. It is a most adaptable animal and is as much at home in a London flat as in a country cottage or a mud hut in Africa. It had its original home somewhere in Asia, but has spread to the other continents.

Mice breed extremely quickly, and one pair can soon produce enough young to make themselves a serious nuisance. It takes about three weeks for a family of mice to be born, and there may be from 1 to 18 young in each litter. One pair of mice can have 30 or 40 babies a year, or more if food is plentiful.

Owl There are very many different kinds of owls. Usually they are only seen dimly in the dusk, for they are active at night, but they are quite unmistakable from their stumpy bodies and round heads. Their eyes are very large and the feathers round them grow so as to form rings which make them look very wise.

Owls are very useful birds, as they destroy great numbers of rats and mice. They hunt these quite silently, for their plumage is so soft that they make no sound when flying. Owls also catch voles, rabbits, worms, insects and birds. They swallow animals such as rats and mice whole, but they cannot digest their bones and fur, so some time after their meal they bring these up in pellets. These are neat little packets of bones wrapped in the tightly packed fur.

The barn owl is a beautiful orange-buff and grey colour on the upper parts, with white under parts and face. When seen on the wing at dusk it looks quite ghost-like. The tawny owl is the largest of the British owls, being about 38 centimetres long. It is a stout bird with reddish-brown upper parts and buff under parts, both marked with dark brown.

Rabbit The rabbit can be distinguished from the hare by its smaller size and the fact that it has no black tips on its ears. Its general colour is brown with white beneath. The scut, or short tail, has a splash of white on it which serves as a warning signal when a rabbit, outside its burrow with other rabbits, senses danger and bolts down its burrow. Many burrows are made close together and known as warrens.

Rat Rats are rodents, or gnawing animals, and are found in nearly every part of the world. In Great Britain there are two quite different kinds of rats, and they have never been known to interbreed. They are the house rat or black rat, and the brown rat. Their names are inaccurate and their colours are not a reliable way of telling them apart.

Both kinds have come from the East. They got into ships in Eastern ports and escaped from them when they anchored in England. The black rat was the first to arrive and may have come in the ships bringing crusaders home during the 11th, 12th and 13th centuries. It is a better climber than the brown rat and gets into the upper parts of buildings.

The brown rat came much later and apparently reached Europe only at the beginning of the 18th century. It is fond of water and keeps mostly to the ground, travelling through sewers and entering basements.

Robin The boldest and most friendly of British wild birds is the robin. Because of the orange-red feathers of its face, throat and breast it has another name, the redbreast.

Besides gardens, robins are found in hedgerows and woods, feeding on worms, insects and berries. Sometimes they nest in woods, among ivy, or in holes in banks, but they also choose some very strange places in which to bring up their young. They sometimes build their nests in old tins or kettles or even go into outhouses and nest on a shelf or in such odd places as the pocket of a coat and in the saddlebag of an old bicycle.

The nest itself is made of dead leaves and moss and lined with hair. Usually the hen robin lays five or six white eggs, thickly covered with reddish spots.

Snail In all parts of the world, wherever there is vegetation, snails are to be found. They are gastropod molluscs, which means that the underside of the body is flat and strongly muscular, forming a kind of foot. On this foot they glide along, giving off a slime which eventually hardens. The slime helps their movement and is left behind as a glistening trail.

The snail shell is situated a little behind its front, or head, end, and the whole body can be withdrawn into it.

The snail breathes by drawing in air through a small opening near the edge of the shell, to one side. Inside the mouth is a ribbon-like tongue covered with rows of tiny teeth, and the snail uses this as a rasp to break up its food, which in most cases is green or decaying plants. Behind the mouth are two pairs of tentacles, or feelers. At the tip of the back pair are the eyes, and when the snail is not using these it withdraws them under its shell.